CHARLES T. MCBIDDLE

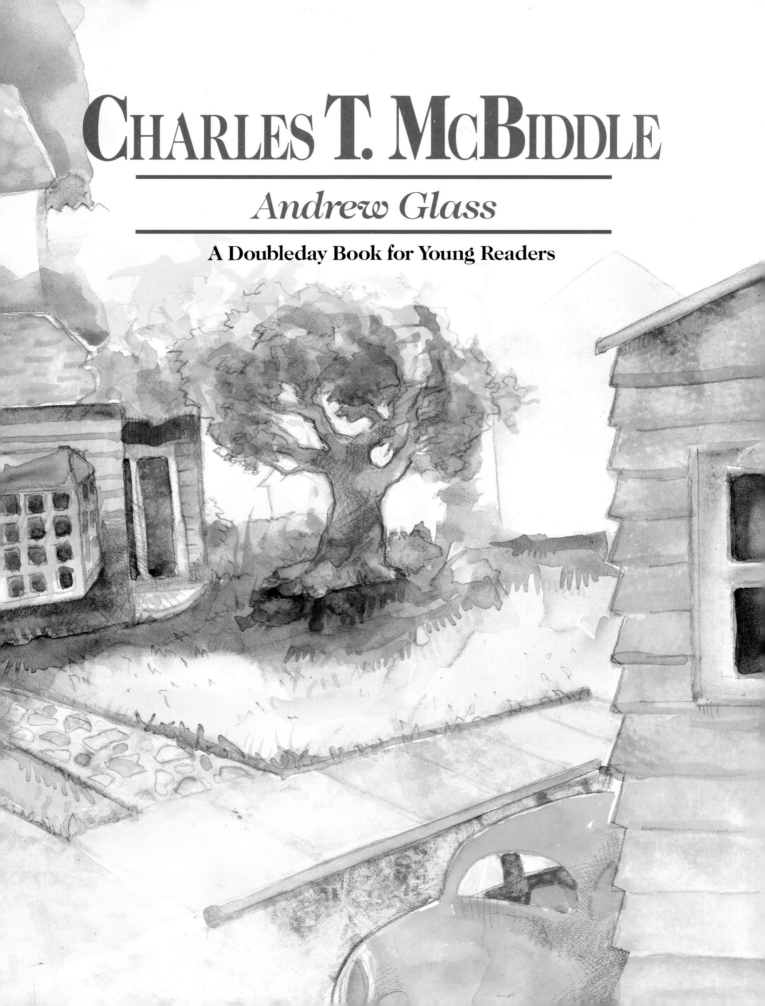

CHARLES T. MCBIDDLE

Andrew Glass

A Doubleday Book for Young Readers

A DOUBLEDAY BOOK FOR YOUNG READERS
Published by
Delacorte Press
Bantam Doubleday Dell Publishing Group, Inc.
666 Fifth Avenue
New York, New York 10103
Doubleday and the portrayal of an anchor
with a dolphin are trademarks of
Bantam Doubleday Dell Publishing Group, Inc.
Copyright © 1993 by Andrew Glass

Library of Congress
Cataloging in Publication Data
Glass, Andrew.
Charles T. McBiddle / written and
illustrated by Andrew Glass.
        p.   cm.
Summary: Charles T. McBiddle persists in
trying to learn to ride his bike, despite a
nasty little creature's attempt to undermine
his confidence.
ISBN 0-385-30554-0
[1. Bicycles and bicycling—Fiction.
2. Self-confidence—Fiction.]   I. Title.
PZ7.G48115Cg   1993
[E]—dc20   91-29026   CIP   AC

Manufactured in Hong Kong

February 1993

10   9   8   7   6   5   4   3   2   1

SCP

To my father

It was a beautiful day on Escarpment Avenue. Charles Tarzan McBiddle unscrewed the training wheels from the back of his bicycle—first the left, then the right. The kickstand kept the bike upright.

"When I can ride
like other kids
my father will say,
'Charles Tarzan
is nobody's fool.'

"My mother will say,
'Anyone who can ride a bike
like that must be on his way.'
"George Batman will say,
'I'm proud to be your brother.'"

Charles Tarzan kicked up the kickstand. He knew how to get on with a push and a jump...but it was not as easy as it looked.

He fell over. "Nothing is holding this stupid bike up," he muttered.

He tried again. Again he fell over. "This is impossible," he said.

"Maybe you should give up," piped a small voice.

"What?" exclaimed Charles Tarzan, turning to see who was there.

"Maybe you're still too little,"
said a tiny creature,
who looked like a very ugly chipmunk.
"Your mother thinks so."

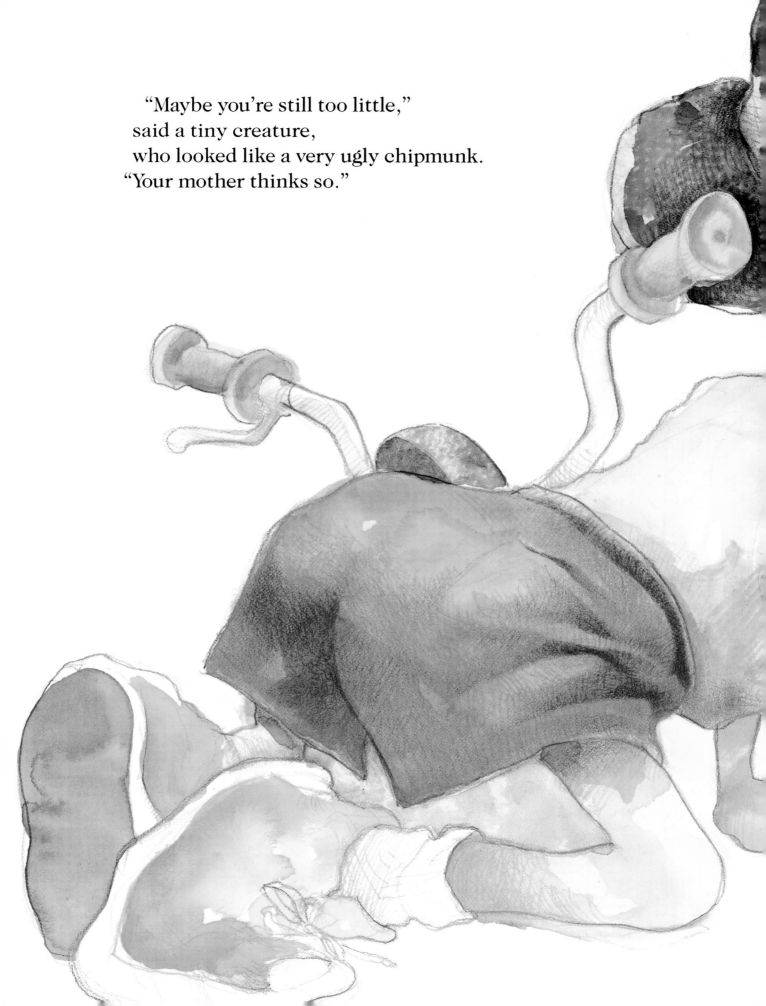

"How do you know?" asked
Charles Tarzan.
"Oh, she told me herself,"
replied the creature confiden-
tially. As it spoke, it grew
larger.

"Your dad told me he doesn't think you're quite
ready yet," it continued boldly, growing still bigger.
"But I stuck up for you, Charlie. I said, 'Oh well, Mr.
McBiddle, it's not so important.'"

The beast put its arm around Charles Tarzan.
It was smoking a huge cigar. "By the way, Charlie,
George Batman thinks you're a dope," it said,
blowing foul smoke right in Charles Tarzan's face.

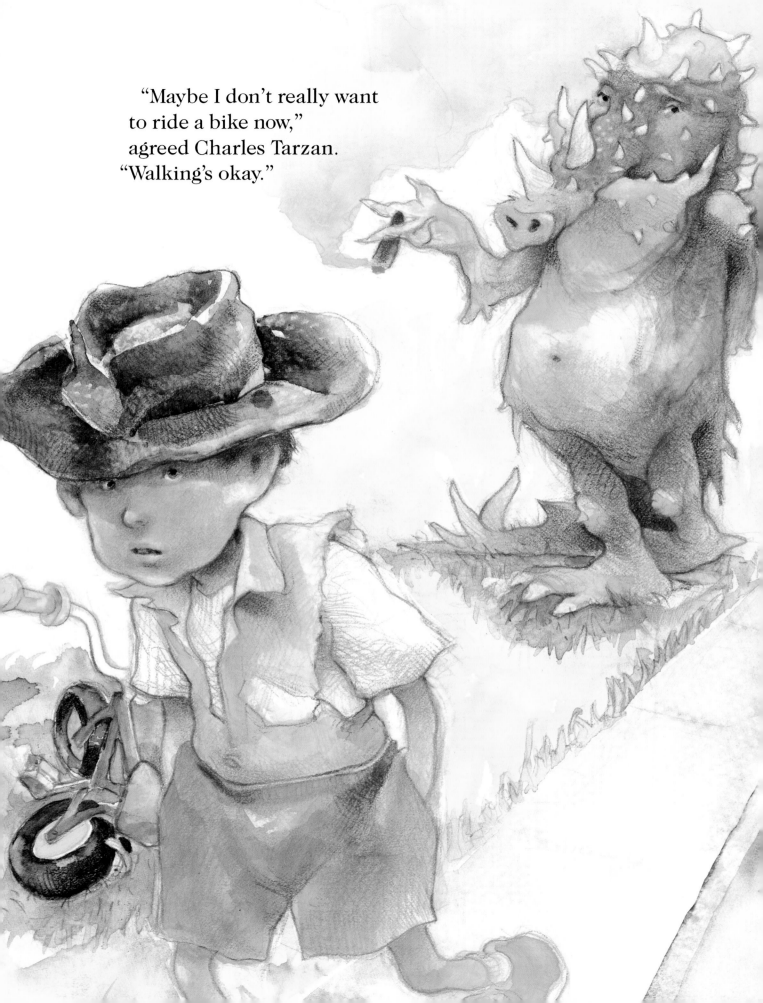

"Maybe I don't really want
to ride a bike now,"
agreed Charles Tarzan.
"Walking's okay."

By now the creature had grown into a huge beast. It danced gaily around Charles Tarzan, clapping its hairy hands and singing, "Impossible, impossible, impossible."

Charles Tarzan sat in the grass watching the drooling beast. "Why don't we go inside and watch television?" it suggested.

"I'm going to try again,"
said Charles Tarzan McBiddle.
  Then the beast turned mean.
  "A kid who can't even
get on his bike by himself
had better watch
what he says,"
it sneered.

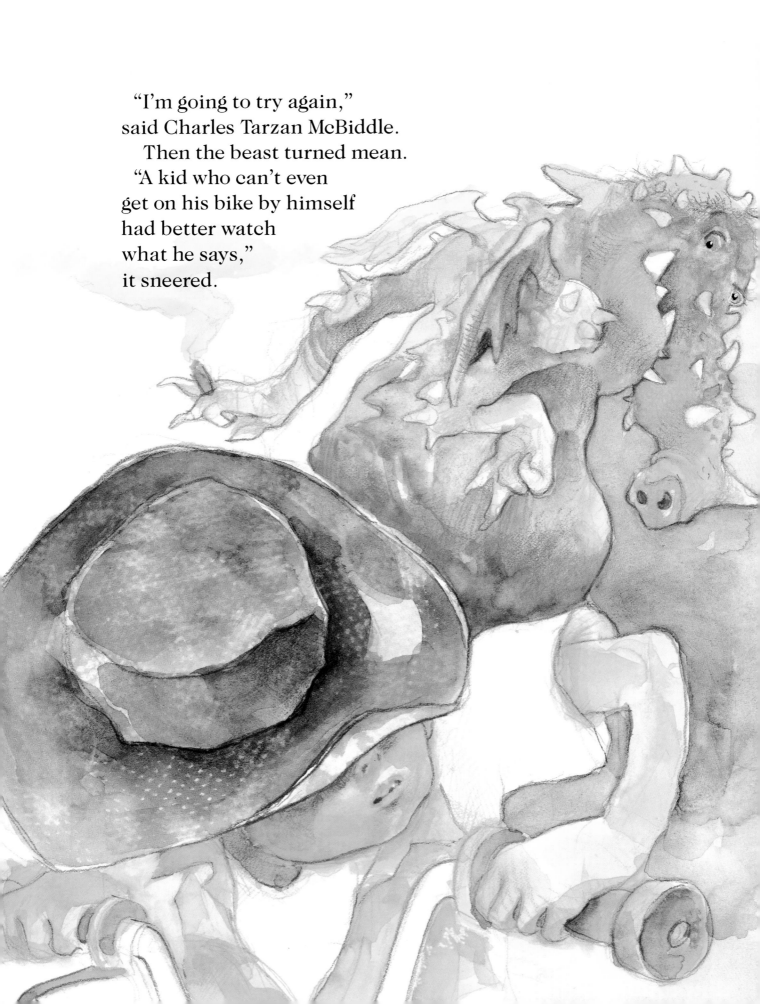

Charles Tarzan picked
himself and his bike up
from the grass. When he
jumped on, the monster
leapt on too.

Charles Tarzan and the monster both fell over.
Bigger and uglier than before, it growled, "You're
wasting your time, Charlie boy."

"Well, I'm going to try again anyway and I'm going to keep on trying," said Charles Tarzan McBiddle.

"Don't say that again," snarled the monster.
"Everyone knows you can't do it. Your mom wishes
you would give up."

"That's not true!" shouted Charles Tarzan. "You're
a liar."

"So what?"
laughed the monster.

"So this," replied Charles Tarzan, and he picked
up his bike again. The monster shriveled a little.
"Oh yeah?" it spat.

"Oh yeah!" said Charles Tarzan, jumping on his bike and pedaling wildly. The wrinkled beast held on tight. But this time they rode a few feet before falling over.

"You see!" exclaimed Charles Tarzan.

"Big deal," snarled the monster. "A few lousy inches."

"I'll make it to the maple tree this time," said Charles Tarzan.

But he didn't.
"You'd better try harder if you want your dad to like you," shrieked the shrunken, shriveling beast.

"My father loves me," shouted Charles Tarzan, and this time he made it all the way to the maple tree.

"Your brother,
George Batman,
will still think
you're a dope,"
rasped the creature.

"So what?" replied Charles Tarzan coolly, getting on his bike again. This time the creature couldn't hold on any longer. It tumbled off as Charles Tarzan sped away on his bike.

"Isn't that the victory cry of the great ape I hear?" asked Mrs. McBiddle.

Mr. McBiddle answered, "Charles Tarzan must have learned to ride his bicycle."

About the author and illustrator

Andrew Glass has illustrated more than thirty books for children, some of which he has written himself, including the Spooky series by Natalie Savage Carlson and *Larger Than Life* by Robert San Souci. He lives in New York City.

About the book

The illustrations for this book were created with Pelican watercolor paints and Caran D'Ache Supracolor No. 2 pencils applied to Strathmore illustration board.

 The book is set in 16-point ITC Caslon No. 224. The typography is by Lynn Braswell.